For Charlie, J. S.

For Greta, Emilio and Loveday,
from Grumpy Trousers, R. A.

First published in Great Britain by HarperCollins Children's Books in 2004
First published in paperback in 2005

1 3 5 7 9 10 8 6 4 2

ISBN: 0-00-710394-8

Text copyright © James Sage 2004
Illustrations copyright © Russell Ayto 2004

HarperCollins Children's Books is a division of HarperCollins Publishers Ltd.
The author and illustrator assert the moral right to be identified
as the author and illustrator of the work.
A CIP catalogue record for this title is available from the British Library.

Visit our website at: www.harpercollinschildrensbooks.co.uk

Printed and bound in Singapore

Mr Beast

James Sage

illustrated by Russell Ayto

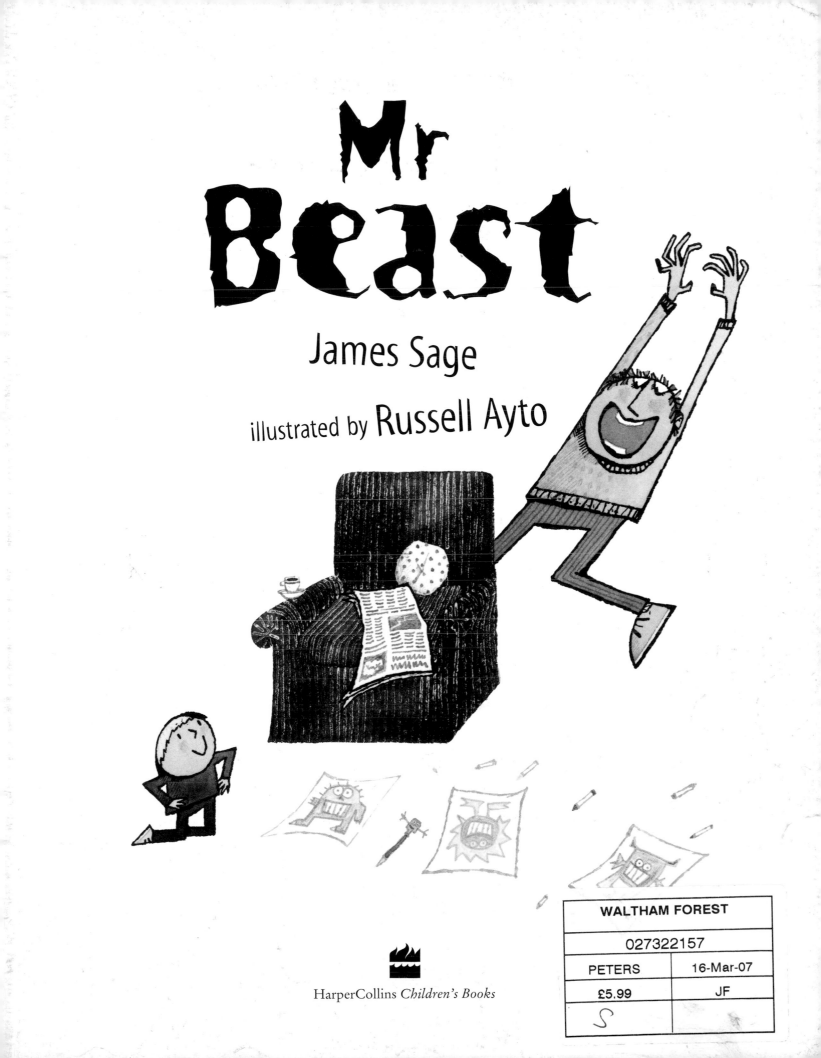

HarperCollins *Children's Books*

Charlie loved monsters almost as much as he loved sugared doughnuts. Which is why his mum said to him one day: Charlie my pet, if I had a larger frying pan, I'd make some of your favourite sugared doughnuts. Go and ask Mr Beast if I can borrow his big old black one.

So Charlie set off down the garden.

With pleasure! gushed Mr Beast,

picking his ugly sharp teeth with a

twing and a **twang**

But tell your dear mother that I

expect to have my big old black

pan returned filled to the brim

with her delectable doughnuts!

So Charlie lugged the frying pan
home and his mum made him as
many doughnuts as he could eat
(which was a lot!).

Then she made a batch for Mr Beast which Charlie lugged back.

But on the way, Charlie began to eat these doughnuts, too…

and he kept on eating them...

until there was only one pathetic

little doughnut left.

And then he ate

THAT!

It's my sweet tooth, explained
Charlie. But such a lame excuse
did not satisfy Mr Beast.

You've eaten all my doughnuts,
bozo, so tonight I'll eat you!
Depend upon it!
And then he slammed the door
with a BANG!

When Charlie told his mum
that Mr Beast was planning to
eat him, she said she was very
sorry indeed to hear that as
she would miss him terribly
but would try not to fret.

Then Charlie went through the house…

…and checking to see that Mr Beast…

...locking all the doors...   and shutting all the windows...

...wasn't already lurking in the broom cupboard, or hiding behind the fish tank.

Not long afterwards Charlie went
to bed . . . but not to sleep! For it
was then that Mr Beast came
visiting, just as he said he would!

I'm going to eat you up,
Charlie boy, he called.
I'm outside now!

Shuffle

Rumble

Grunt!

And Charlie could hear
Mr Beast clambering up
the creeper!

Crickle

Crackle

Crunch!

And then Charlie could hear
Mr Beast clattering about
on the roof!

Piddle

Paddle

Plunk!

I'm coming to
eat you up,
yes I am!

And then Charlie could hear
Mr Beast stuffing himself
into the chimney!

Squiggle

Shimmy...

And then sliding down it!

swish
Slither...

SLUMP!

Now I'm in the
house and I'm really
going to eat you up!
he shouted.

And Charlie could hear
Mr Beast stomping
along the hall!

Then Charlie heard
Mr Beast kick open the
bedroom door with one
mighty thrust of his
great big foot!

And walk right in!

Blim

Blam

BLUMP!

And when Charlie
heard this he did what
any brave person would
do in the circumstances.
He made himself
as little as
possible.

YEEEhaw!

howled Mr Beast as he yanked
back the bedcovers. And now I
really and truly will EAT YOU UP!

And he tickled Charlie all over
while roaring in a very
beastly voice, YUM!
YUMMY! YUM!
As Charlie shouted,
BUT IT'S ONLY
ME, DADDY,
IT'S ONLY
ME!

Such a racket naturally brought Charlie's mum hurrying upstairs. And this is only me to tell you both that's quite enough silliness for one evening! she announced.

She told Charlie's daddy to act his age if he possibly could, as it was already way past Charlie's bedtime…

...and Charlie to stop dwelling on sugared doughnuts and go to sleep without delay!

And they both promised to be as good as gold from that moment on.

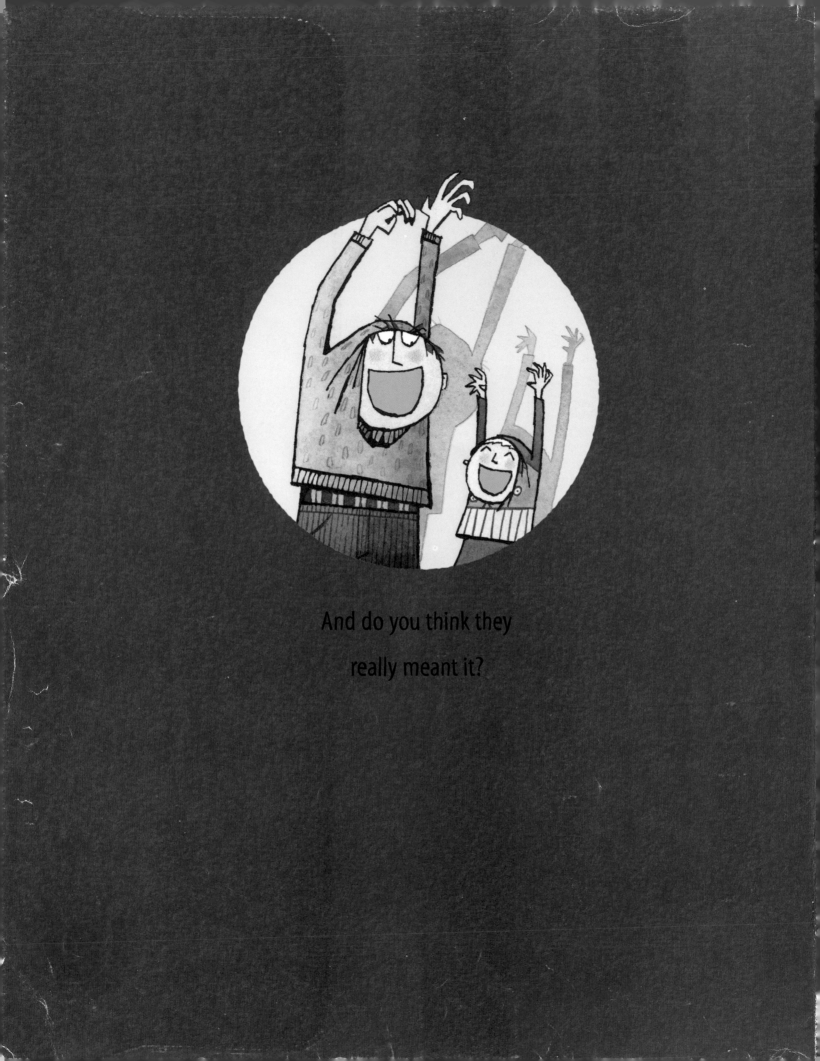

And do you think they

really meant it?